D1442556

Other Lothrop, Lee & Shepard Books
by Jan Ormerod
Sunshine, Moonlight, Rhymes Around the Day,
101 Things to Do with a Baby

For Judy

Library of Congress Cataloging in Publication Data
Ormerod, Jan.
Dad's back.
(Jan Ormerod's Baby books)
Summary: Dad comes home and plays with baby.
1. Children's stories, English. [1. Babies—Fiction. 2. Fathers—Fiction] I. Title.
II. Series: Ormerod, Jan. Baby books.
PZ7.0634Dad   1985   [E]   84-12614
ISBN 0-688-04126-4

Dad's Back

Jan Ormerod

LOTHROP, LEE & SHEPARD BOOKS
NEW YORK

Dad's back
with jingling keys,

warm gloves,

a cold nose,

a long,
long scarf,

and apples in a bag.

Dad's back
with a game,

a chase,

and a tickle.

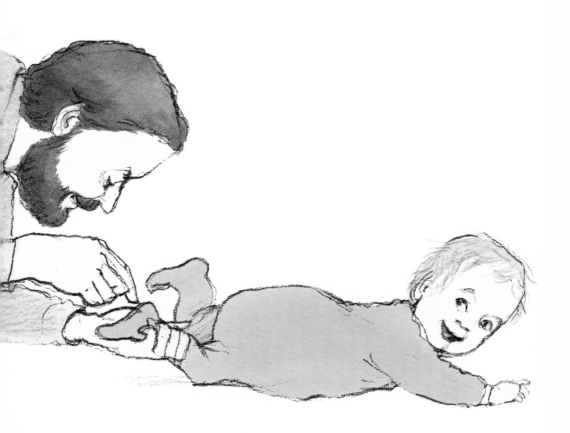

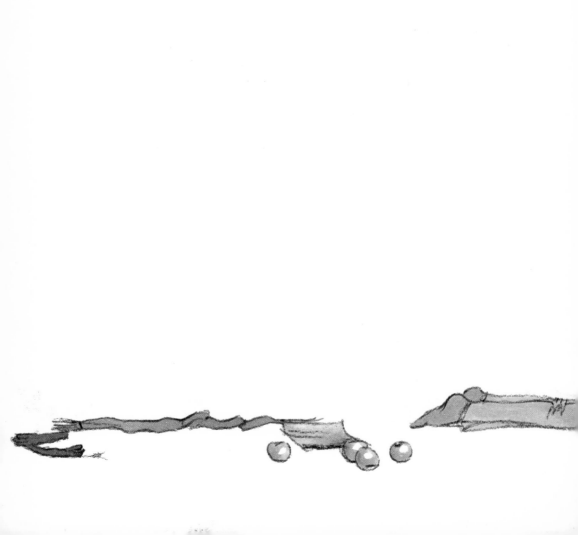